Mia
The Sweetest Valentine

HarperFestival is an imprint of HarperCollins Publishers.
Mia: The Sweetest Valentine

www.harpercollinschildrens.com
Library of Congress catalog card number: 2012934641
ISBN 978-0-06-210012-2
Book design by Sean Boggs
12 13 14 15 16   LEO   10 9 8 7 6 5 4 3 2 1   ❖   First Edition

Mia
The Sweetest Valentine

HARPER FESTIVAL

An Imprint of HarperCollinsPublishers

By Robin Farley • Pictures by Olga and Aleksey Ivanov

DING DONG!
Mia danced to the front door in her pink-and-red tutu.
"Happy Valentine's Day!" she said.
"Happy Valentine's Day!" replied Anna and Ruby.

Mia handed her friends sparkly tiaras. "Let's go to my room," she said. "I decorated for our party!"

"Mia," Mrs. Cat chimed in, "I'm going to the store now, but your dad is in the study if you need anything!"

"Thanks, Mama!" Mia replied.

Anna, Ruby, and Mia went upstairs. Mia's room was decorated with balloons, paper hearts, and streamers.

Ruby and Anna pulled out valentines for each of their friends.
"Where are your valentines, Mia?" asked Anna.
"Oh," said Mia. "They're in the kitchen. I'll go get them."

Mia danced into the kitchen and grabbed her art box from the table.
There was another box on the table, too. It was shiny and shaped like a heart.
"Oh! Yum!" she said. "Chocolates!"

Mia ran back upstairs to her friends. "Look what I found," she said, holding up the box of chocolates.

"What is it?" asked Ruby.

"Valentine chocolates!" said Mia. "Let's open them."

"Are you sure that's okay?" asked Ruby.
"Well," Mia said. "Everyone should have chocolates on Valentine's Day!"
Before she could change her mind, Mia opened up the box.

"Which one would you like?" Mia asked Ruby.

Ruby picked a chocolate heart.

Anna picked a piece with a pink heart on it.

Mia held up the largest chocolate in the box and popped it in her mouth.

"Tumph frumph valentumphs!" said Anna, with a mouth full of chocolate.
"What?!" asked Mia and Ruby.
Anna swallowed. "Time for valentines!" she exclaimed. The girls all giggled.

Anna gave valentines decorated with stickers. Mia passed out cards with famous ballerinas on them. Ruby had made her own valentines. She drew pictures of Mia and Anna dancing.

Mia reached for another chocolate, but they were all gone!

"Oh no!" said Mia. "We ate the whole box!"

"It's okay, Mia," replied Ruby. "Want to go make up a new dance now?"

"Yes!" Anna and Mia shouted, racing out of Mia's room.

The girls pranced to the den, leaving the empty box of chocolates on the floor.

Later on, after Ruby and Anna had gone home, Mr. Cat came into Mia's room.
"Mia!" Mr. Cat called. "Have you seen a heart-shaped box of chocolates?"
"Yes," said Mia. "It was on the kitchen table."

"Where is it now?" he asked.

"We ate them at the Valentine's Day party," replied Mia.

Mr. Cat frowned. "That box was your mom's Valentine's Day present."

Mia felt terrible. "I'm sorry," she said. "I didn't know."

Mr. Cat hugged Mia. "It's okay. But now I need your help. We need to think of a new gift for your mom."

Mr. Cat and Mia made a list of ideas: flowers, a cake, candy. But Mia's mom would be home soon. It was too late to buy a new present!

Mia looked around her room. She saw the valentine Ruby had given her. Suddenly, Mia had an idea.

"I know!" she said. "Mama loves to watch me dance. We can put on a Valentine's Day show!"

"Great idea!" said Mr. Cat. "But you will have to give me some dance tips."

Mia smiled.

Mia and Mr. Cat set up a little theater in the living room. They practiced and practiced. Mia taught Mr. Cat how to twirl. She showed him how to leap and point his toes.

Soon, they heard the front door open. "I'm home!" called Mrs. Cat.
"In here!" said Mia. "We have a present for you!"

Mr. Cat escorted Mrs. Cat to her seat.
"Welcome to your special Valentine's Day show!" said Mia, taking a bow.
Mia started the music. Mr. Cat and Mia twirled and leaped.
They spun and walked on their toes.
They were wonderful!

Mrs. Cat clapped and cheered.

"Bravo!" she said. "That was the best Valentine's Day present ever! I have a present for you both, too—though mine couldn't possibly be as delightful."

Mrs. Cat pulled a heart-shaped box of chocolates from her purse.

Mia and Mr. Cat couldn't help but giggle.

Mia, Ruby, and Anna exchange valentines, and so can you with your friends! Trace the template below onto as many pieces of paper as you want. Then cut the paper valentines out, fold them in half, and decorate them using the stickers inside this book. Don't forget to write "To" and "From" on the outside of the valentine. Happy Valentine's Day!